"In the twenty-first century, we are still questioning 'who is our neighbor?' Unger shows us in *The Good Neighbor* just how much our world is fractured by indifference. Who among us has the compassion to reach out to our neighbors during their struggles and challenges?"

—**Kathleen Seagreaves**, Retired

"*The Good Neighbor* is a poignant reminder of how God's love and grace can be explored and embraced in the deepest parts of our spirits and hearts. This retelling of the Parable of the Good Samaritan brought tears of joy, sorrow, faith, and hope for the ongoing transformation of our spiritual lives. Unger has captured the essence of God's grace and the intersections of God's grace with our world, while reminding us of the deeper love and relationship we are called to with our neighbors—all beloved of God."

—**Bonnie Bates**, Conference Minister, Retired

"Dr. Peter Unger is a marvelous storyteller. In *The Good Neighbor*, Peter takes up the Parable of the Good Samaritan—crafted by possibly the most consummate storyteller of all time, Jesus—and breathes new life into it. The original story is found in Luke 10:27–37, where a lawyer approaches Jesus with an earnest desire to inherit eternal life. He understands the two greatest commandments, but he wants to know precisely who his neighbor is. In this fresh retelling, we are taken right where we expect to go—to see that one's neighbor is not defined by proximity or relationship, but rather 'being merciful' to someone in need. We are rewarded for making this journey with a delightful and enlightening ending!"

—**Blake Heffner**, Lecturer in Philosophy and Religion,
Penn State Lehigh Valley

"Peter B. Unger's *The Good Neighbor* is a quiet but pointed work of Christian fiction that revisits one of the most familiar parables in the Gospels and asks readers to hear it again as though for the first time. . . . It takes a familiar biblical teaching and restores to it its unsettling power. Unger has written a thoughtful, compassionate, and timely novel that challenges legalistic faith without abandoning conviction."

—**Michael Friedman**, Editor, *Skope Magazine*

The Good Neighbor

The Good Neighbor

Peter B. Unger

RESOURCE *Publications* • Eugene, Oregon

THE GOOD NEIGHBOR

Resource Publications
An Imprint of Wipf and Stock Publishers
199 W. 8th Ave., Suite 3
Eugene, OR 97401

www.wipfandstock.com

PAPERBACK ISBN: 979-8-3852-7577-9
HARDCOVER ISBN: 979-8-3852-7578-6
EBOOK ISBN: 979-8-3852-7579-3

VERSION NUMBER 03/17/26

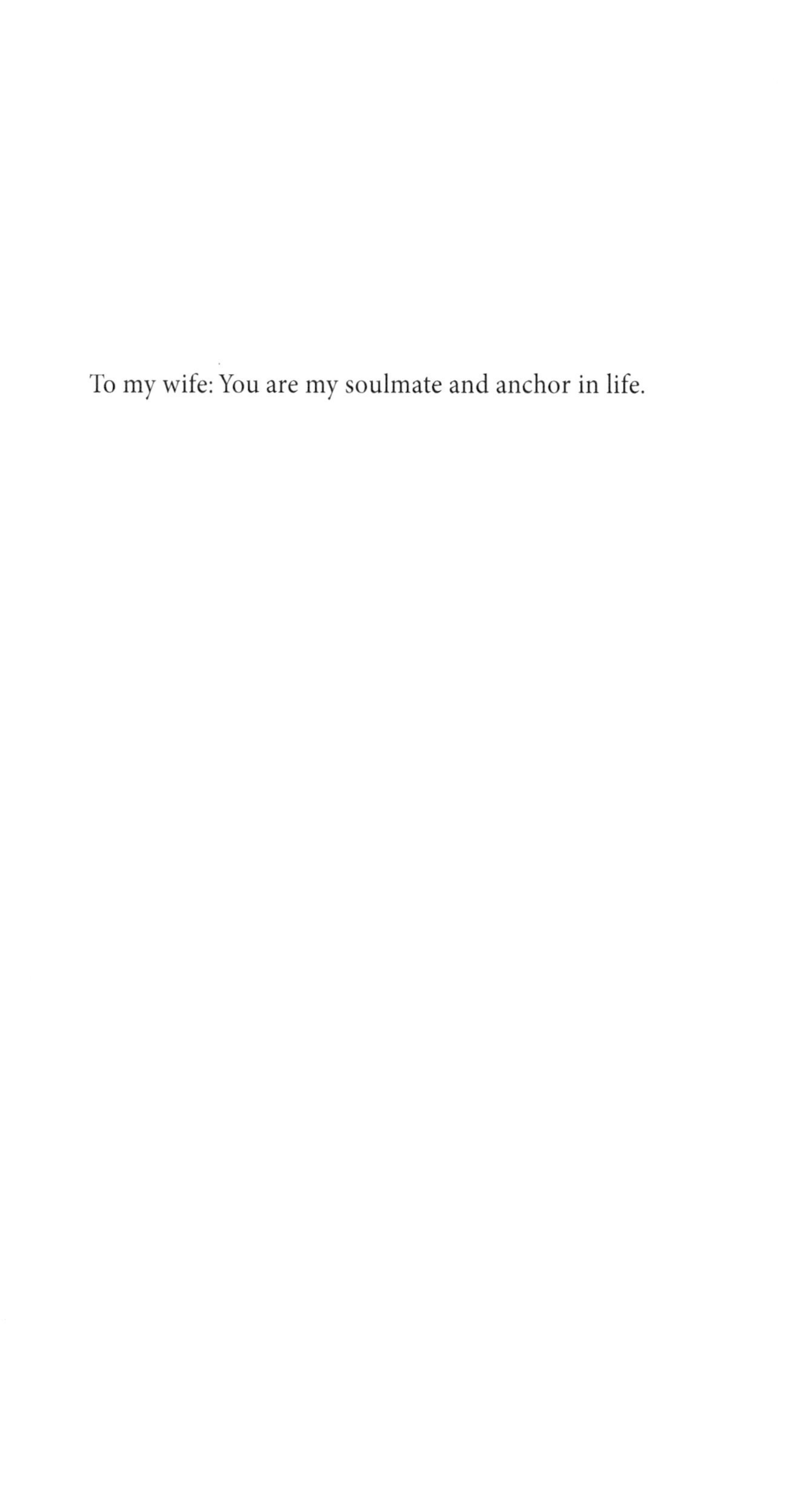

To my wife: You are my soulmate and anchor in life.

Contents

The Question

It was not an Advent sermon. It alluded to Advent themes, but its text, Luke 10:25–37, was hardly appropriate for the Advent season. At the coffee hour in the fellowship hall after the service, whispering could be heard among more than a few. "Why," they questioned, "would the pastor preach on the Parable of the Good Samaritan during Advent?" Not only was this not an Advent text, but in past years the pastor had preached on a related series of Advent texts. There was one clue. A few on the governing committee had overheard congregants, including a fellow committee member, complain about the ethnic and religious backgrounds of some of those about to join the church. They suspected the sermon was the pastor's attempt to respond to and reprimand such murmurings. The new members' class included an engaged couple who had been lifelong Roman Catholics but had recently left the tradition for reasons unknown. Also included was a large family with Mexican ancestry who had been attending regularly and now sought to join.

Anti-Mexican, anti-immigrant rhetoric, particularly in certain parts of the country, was at a fever pitch. Over time the pastor had heard members air their suspicions and fears about the influence that Roman Catholic converts, or those marrying into their tradition, might have on their long-held Protestant faith traditions. The pastor suspected that this was due in part to the relaxing of ethnic ties and other boundaries between faith traditions, and in part to the reactionary entrenchment of those members.

In the corner of the large fellowship hall, at a table farthest from the kitchen counter laden with baked goods and a couple of large coffee urns, sat two men, their heads lowered and bowed toward one another in serious private conversation. Both were elders on the church's governing committee. The young man regarded the older man sitting across from him as a spiritual mentor. Knowing this, the gray-haired, bespectacled older man had tolerated the younger man's tendency to express his views in rigidly black-and-white terms. Nowhere was this more evident to him than when the younger man expressed his religious views. This was somewhat offset, however, by the faith questions the young man would ask the older man from time to time in an inquisitive tone and manner.

Raised by parents who were lifelong members of the church, the young man shared their investment in the building and institutional church. Like them he favored the dogmas and doctrines of his faith tradition to the point of being outspokenly legalistic about their acceptance and affirmation by members. At a recent governing committee meeting he had argued vehemently that all those seeking to become members should affirm their allegiance to the black-and-white dogmatic questions posed by the elders before being allowed to join. The younger man had also exhibited a thinly veiled prejudice when he raised objections to the family with Mexican ethnicity becoming members. "They're from such a different background, I am not sure they're a good fit for our church. The parents' English is not the best. I can't understand what they're saying half the time. Besides, we should make sure they're American citizens before allowing them to join." The pastor's stony silence and disapproving scowl prompted the other committee members to deflect the discussion to another issue facing the committee.

The older man knew he had his work cut out for him if a seed was to be planted in the young man where a more personal, authentic, living relationship with Christ might germinate and grow. Perhaps, he thought, this aberrant sermon during Advent might, if skillfully explained, offer him a critical faith lesson. The older man prayed silently for the Holy Spirit to use him to plant this seed of a deeper, living faith in the young man.

Moments earlier, when they'd first sat down, the young man had posed a question about one word in the text. "I've never understood what Jesus meant by 'neighbor' in that passage. While I am sure he wasn't just referring to our next-door neighbor, Jesus certainly couldn't have meant to include everyone else. How would that meet any definition of neighbor? Don't you think he was referring to those we associate with most, our family and friends? Realistically those are the people we spend the most time with, so it stands to reason that they are the ones who would benefit most from this teaching. Even if we extended what Jesus meant by neighbor beyond family and friends, aren't there other greater loyalties that should come first? Don't we have a responsibility toward those fellow Americans who share our country's most cherished patriotic, and I might add Christian, values?"

The older man was aware that he was conflating faith, politics, and patriotism. He was keenly aware of key Gospel texts where Jesus had warned against this. There was Mark 12:17 where Jesus said, "Give to Caesar what is Caesar's and give to God's what is God's," intimating that our very lives, greatest loyalty, and worship belong to God. Then there was John 18:36, where Jesus says to Pilate, "My Kingdom is not of this world."

Clearly Jesus was distinguishing here between political/military earthly powers, and his kingdom, which represents a spiritual reality over against a worldly one. If these were not enough, there was Jesus' admonition in Matthew 24 that his kingdom is destined to "clash" or "collide" with evil earthly powers and kingdoms. In those times power, greed, and false messiahs will stand in increasingly marked contrast to the spiritual integrity of his spiritual kingdom.

The older man was intuitively aware that confronting the younger man's fallacious understandings head-on would be counterproductive. It would likely only create tension between them and throw up a roadblock to their developing friendship. He was also sure, knowing something of the young man's background, that his prejudice and scriptural misunderstandings were driven not only by indoctrinating influences in his life but by the emotional investments they had habituated.

Pausing to take sip a from the Styrofoam cup of coffee in his hand, the older man looked calmly, and with intention, directly into the younger man's eyes. "By way of answering your question and your confusion here, let me recount a story someone once told me." His voice conveyed the gravitas of an older person with much life experience, some of it hard-earned.

The older man then paused and thought to himself for a moment. Realizing that the story he was about to share was long and would keep them sitting there well after the coffee hour ended, he suggested a change of venue. Addressing the young man and sharing this concern, he offered to drive them to a nearby café where he could share the story in a more conducive setting. Once there and with coffee in hand, they settled into a comfortable booth at the uncrowded café where customers often lingered, and after lighter conversational exchanges, the older man began to tell his story.

"This is a true story that took place quite a while back," he began. "It occurred on Christmas Eve, and the experience was both traumatic and marked a transformative turning point in a young man's life. The young man's name was Arlen." He then proceeded to tell the story, including details that Arlen would only learn later about a traumatic, life-altering experience he had. Arlen learned, be it by twist of fate or providence, in the months following his experience, that key characters in the story belonged to the same large downtown church as him. Other members and the pastor had helped inform him about these details. The most important figure in the story, however, was not a member of Arlen's church. She was in fact very unlike Arlen and the other characters, but without her this story cannot be told.

The Old Man's Story

Mireya's Choice

As with any good story I must start at the beginning, and so it is to Mireya and the events that led to the pivotal role she plays that I turn next. It was early evening that Christmas Eve, and Mireya Zelaya Portillo was tired. It was, however, a good tired. Mireya took pride in completing an honest day's work even when it ran long. She had grown accustomed to days that often stretched to nine or ten hours, clearing and cleaning tables at the diner. Her bussing job required her to be in constant motion. Lifting and carrying the heavy dish-laden bussing tubs back to the dishwasher in the kitchen had often made her shoulders and back ache by nightfall. In her early forties, she was still young and healthy enough to endure the back-breaking work, although an occasional shooting pain in her back reminded Mireya she was not as young as she once was.

Given her broken English, the Greek restaurant owner initially had qualms about hiring her two years earlier, but her warm, shy smile, gentle nature, and repeated refrain "I am a hard worker" had won him over by the interview's end. His positive intuition about Mireya soon proved true. Despite her humble role, olive complexion, and obvious immigrant status, she later showed him her green card, she quickly became a favorite among the staff and an increasing number of regular patrons. It was the late 1990s and anti-immigrant prejudice, particularly toward certain nationalities, religions, and ethnicities, was on the rise. Coming to know Mireya personally was all it took for those who harbored such prejudices to disregard these, at least with her.

The endearing smile, and humble manner with which she asked if it was okay to remove empty dishes had won these customers over, and they began interacting with her on a more personal level. They would ask her name and where she was from in an interested and caring way. "Honduras," she would reply. Other interactions would follow in subsequent visits, and as these patrons came to know Mireya better they grew fonder of her. Upon being seated, if they saw her pass by they would call out, "Hi, Mireya." Before long some would be asking her how to say expressions like "How are you?" and "I am fine" in Spanish. "¿Cómo estás?" and "Estoy bien," she would respond, happy to oblige. Something about their openness to learning a few phrases in Spanish helped bridge their two cultures. It also affirmed her hope and desire to become an American would be accepted, even encouraged, by them. Having to learn English, she thought to herself, in a nation founded by immigrants should never disqualify one from becoming a citizen. After all, had many, initially, not struggled to learn English as well?

The diner had been there for over half a century. It had once lain outside the center of the then large town, but in recent decades it had been absorbed by the expanding downtown area of the now medium-sized city. Over time Mireya had even broken down the barriers that existed between her and the older, more conservative long-term customers who still frequented the diner, often from outlying rural areas. Initially some had acted aloof and suspicious when she came to take their dishes away. Gradually, through small interactions, she had been able to win them over. The shy, humble warmth of her smile and engaging manner had gradually broken down their wall of reserve. They came to know her not as an object to project stereotypes onto but as a fellow human being with whom they could have a more personable relationship. She then became known to them simply as Mireya, the warm, friendly individual who helped lift their spirits over breakfast after the aches and pains they felt upon arising had not put them in the best of moods. Now, with Mireya having worked for over two years at the diner, many of the patrons that frequented it did so, partly, in eager anticipation of seeing her.

A couple of weeks earlier, with Christmas approaching, a few patrons who had grown especially fond of Mireya had asked if she would be spending Christmas with family. "No, I live alone," she replied with a wistful smile, unusual for her. Not surprisingly, other questions then followed.

"Did you come to America by yourself?"

"Yes," Mireya replied. "I have a mother, brothers, and sisters back in Honduras. I also have many nieces and nephews. I miss them . . ." Mireya added, searching for the right words, "very, very much at this time of year." Mireya knew, but did not share, the family's daily struggles to overcome the poverty, gang violence, and general lawlessness that infested the part of Honduras where she had lived.

Like so many immigrants before, they began to place their hopes for a better life, at least for some family members, in a country that seemed even farther away than it was, called America. They knew if someone in the family could gain a legal foothold there, this would offer a better chance for other family members to emigrate.

As the only one of her siblings that was unmarried, Mireya, against the fears and protests of her family, had decided she was the best one in the family to attempt the journey to America. Her extended family members had scraped together the money needed for Mireya to make this difficult and dangerous journey. If granted asylum, she hoped to earn and save enough money to send some back to her family in Honduras. Once at the border, she had applied for asylum and had received it conditionally. She had come armed with records and family letters citing the rampant crime activity where she had lived in Honduras.

She had also shared records disclosing the deaths of two young male extended family members at the hands of gang members with whom they had been uncooperative. After one year, and having secured a job, she had applied for a green card, and after the required waiting period it had been granted. Mireya knew how complicated immigration laws could be and continually thanked God that she had come this far. She did not know what the future held and dared not start the naturalization process yet. This was partly due to a goal she had set for herself to speak English more fluently in hopes of performing better during this process. She remained determined to adhere to the complicated and confusing legal process of becoming an American, including court appearances and paperwork, as best she could.

The couple inquiring about how she would spend Christmas, detecting the longing sadness in Mireya's voice, deflected the conversation to another line of questioning. "We know you don't drive, Mireya. Do you live nearby?"

"Only a mile or two away. I live in a . . . I think you call it a brownstone."

"Oh, how nice," the wife responded disingenuously, knowing full well that this Brownstone neighborhood had gone downhill in recent decades and was now regarded as being in an area with a higher crime rate.

What Mireya, understandably, did not share was that she lived in a small one-bedroom basement apartment with a window that looked out onto the sidewalk. Mireya had decorated this small apartment as best she could. Entering the apartment, one would walk down a short hallway and find themself in the main living area. It was a square space just large enough for the small couch, worn upholstered chair, side table, and the standing lamp next to it that the room contained. She had purchased the furniture secondhand. To further warm up the apartment she had laid down a colorful square-shaped rug that covered most of the floor. Most of the wall hangings displayed artwork from her native land. Pictures of family cluttered the front of the table by the chair. A large calendar that hung on the wall across the room, near a small kitchenette, was conspicuously different from all the other wall decorations. The pictures, which corresponded to the months of the year, were of famous American symbols and landmarks that included the American flag and the Statue of Liberty.

A small free-standing oil heater sat in front of the couch. Toward the back of the side table, between the armchair and couch, Mireya had placed a small fake Christmas tree she had purchased. Mireya had decorated it with Christmas lights, garlands of popcorn and cranberries she had made, and Christmas baubles she had bought weeks earlier. A waitress with whom Mireya was particularly close had given her an early Christmas gift: a simple, small olive wood nativity set that included just Mary, Joseph and baby Jesus. It sat in front of the small Christmas tree on the side table under the standing lamp, and between the armchair and the tree. Whenever Mireya looked at the nativity set, she experienced something of an otherworldly hope, comfort, and sense of belonging that transcended her precarious status as an immigrant and outsider in America.

Mireya had allowed herself two luxuries. One was the TV that sat on a stand across from the easy chair, and to the left of the entrance to the kitchenette area. She had bought it to augment her English lessons out of the basic *How to Speak English* book written for Spanish speakers that she was studying. The other was the flip phone she had purchased. Not having a car and having to walk to work and back home at the end of the day, she felt more secure carrying this on her, especially in case of an emergency.

The couple had shared with Mireya that it was snowing heavily outside and wished her a safe walk home. With her shift over Mireya went back to the kitchen to retrieve her coat. Saying goodbye to staff members, she put her coat on and braced herself for the walk home. While she looked forward to curling up on her small couch in front of the oil heater and enjoying a cup of tea before heading to bed, she always experienced anxiety anticipating the walk home. Although the way home did not take her through the worst section of the greater downtown area, it bordered a crime-ridden area. On one stretch she would have to pass an old industrial area where two large cement parking garages with multiple levels sat just off the main street. Fairly safe and commonly used in the daytime, at night they appeared to be looming, foreboding sentinels warning the passerby of the dangers the area posed. A poorly lit alleyway ran between them and ended on a side street shrouded in shadow due to a lack of streetlights. Mireya knew this offered her a shortcut home, but knowing the long alleyway made her more vulnerable to an attack of some kind, she had chosen to avoid it. Earlier in the day, one of the waitresses had cautioned her to be extra careful, as the morning newspaper had reported that police were investigating a series of muggings in the greater area she had to walk through. Mireya buttoned up her old reddish-brown knee-length coat and, clutching her purse close to her, began her walk home.

The first part of the walk took her past apartment buildings, offices, and storefronts well-lit by streetlights. Soon, however, she approached the dimly lit old industrial area where the streetlights were spaced further apart. Then the two large parking garages came clearly into view on the right side of the street.

Perhaps it was the uplifting ambience that Christmas Eve lent the evening. Or perhaps it was the steadily falling snow that brightened the otherwise dimly lit alleyway. Spotlights had been attached too high to the sidewalls of the garages to provide sufficient lighting. Perhaps it was something more. Whatever it was, Mireya stopped walking, peered down the alleyway, and weighed whether or not to take this shortcut this one time. As she glanced about herself, the snow seemed to cleanse and cheer up this drab, gloomy part of the city and even the long and deserted alleyway. Tired and with her feet and toes beginning to feel numb from the cold, she impulsively decided to chance it. She also felt safer than on other evenings on this holy night that made God's love, embodied in the Christ Child, feel especially close. Saying a brief prayer for the Lord's presence to accompany her, she started making her way down the long, narrow alleyway. The thin red rubber boots she had pulled over her shoes back at the diner had kept her shoes dry. Each step she took made a crunching sound as she walked on the now inch-deep snow. The noise was amplified, for

Mireya, by the alleyway and the slightly menacing stillness of the cold night air.

Prayer had been and still was an integral part of her and her family's life. It had helped see them through many difficult times, their faith instilling in them an otherworldly hope and resilience in the face of overwhelming poverty and threats to safety they dealt with almost daily. With her prayer finished, Mireya now not only felt her courage reinforced but also felt strangely drawn down the alleyway that offered her a shortcut home.

She quickened her steps as the end of the alleyway that opened onto the poorly lit side street came into view. I'll be home on my couch in my warm apartment sooner than usual, she reassured herself. As she came within fifty feet of the end of the alleyway Mireya breathed a sigh of relief, her breath emitting a misty cloud into the cold winter air. The jarring sound of a metal door opening on the right side at the end of the garage, and the sight of a man stepping out into the alleyway, caused a wave of anxiety to sweep over her. Seeing him to be a well-dressed middle-aged businessman who took no notice of her, she breathed another sigh of relief and felt herself begin to relax. She watched him round the corner into the shadows that, like dark gloomy silhouettes, clung to the side street's sidewalk.

A few things then happened in quick succession that seemed to make everything move in slow motion for Mireya and aroused a level of fear within her she had not known since coming to America. Threatening yells peppered with curses, the sounds of a scuffle, the dull thud of someone falling to the ground, and the sound of several individuals running away assailed Mireya's ears. "Oh, dear Lord!" Mireya cried under her breath in panic. Intuitively sensing that the man who had just rounded the corner had been attacked, she followed her terrified utterance with a quick, desperate prayer for him and his family.

Arlen's Journey

Arlen Braker had led a comfortable middle-class, if uneventful, life. He had grown up in the suburbs of the medium-sized city. His father had been a bank manager, his mother a nurse. Arlen, an only child, had grown up attending a local church where his parents were active members. His parents had raised him to believe that adhering to Christian morality was what the Christian religion was most about. As a child, Arlen was quiet and shy and did not like to make waves. He had found, for the most part, the moral rules and boundaries his parents had set for him easy to live with, offering him a sense of structure and security.

His high school years were conventional and not marked by any rebellious phases. While not excelling at either, Arlen had played on the high school baseball team and acted in high school theatrical productions. He had also served on student committees, including the student council. His friends came from similar family backgrounds. After high school, Arlen had been accepted and enrolled at the same state university his parents had attended and where they had met.

At the university, Arlen had decided to major in business and had gone on to become a CPA. Now married with two children of his own, an eight-year-old boy and a ten-year-old girl, he resided with his family in the solidly middle-class suburbs of the rapidly expanding medium-sized city.

Once back home, settled down and married, Arlen sought to instill in his two young children the same Christian values his parents had instilled in him. Seeking to inform himself of the scriptural basis for these values had sparked an interest in Bible study for Arlen. He started attending the weekly Bible study classes the pastor led and began studying the Bible on his own in his spare time. Building on the Ten Commandments, Arlen searched both the Old and New Testaments for verses and passages that informed and underscored the Christian virtues he strived to live his life by: the sanctity of life, marriage and family, sexual morality, self-control, humility, honesty, a work ethic, personal responsibility, and charity among others. Although for him charity had largely been confined to the money pledged to his church, and a few other causes he and his wife supported.

In the Bible studies, Arlen had outspokenly emphasized Christian morality. When the discussion lent itself topically he had attributed the decline of the American family and culture to a loss of Christian values. A degree of self-righteousness became apparent in Arlen's attitude at these times. His pastor strongly suspected that, unwittingly, the Christian faith for Arlen had been reduced to adhering to a set of morals, and Christ to an ethical teacher. He had cautioned him several times in the Bible studies that Christian morals should always be understood through the lens of Jesus' greatest commandment, "to love God with heart, mind, and soul and one's neighbor as oneself." The pastor had made this reference citing the context of the parable of the good Samaritan. Given his investment in Christian morals as that which most defined a Christian, Arlen had never been comfortable with the parable of the good Samaritan. Nor had he been comfortable with Jesus' supreme commandment, inherent in the text, that Jesus taught fulfilled all the Law and the Prophets.

More specifically, he had never understood what Jesus meant by "neighbor," much less his identifying of the Samaritan as the good neighbor. Even the thought of living an authenticating relational life with the living Christ through his transformative love and grace were beyond his comprehension. No life experience Arlen had had up to this point in his life had occasioned such spiritual reflection.

What Arlen could not deny, and what troubled him, was that despite all his moral striving, he knew he was far from perfect. He had often wrestled with insecurities, and nagging faith questions. One of those questions that had aroused a fleeting anxiety within him from time to time was "Will my moral strivings alone be enough for God to reward me with eternal life?" His study of the Bible had largely been confined to searching for all those verses and passages that gave divine sanction to the morals he strove to habituate. He had memorized them—chapter, verse, and content—just in case anyone challenged his understanding of the scriptural basis for these Christian morals.

What Arlen had, semi-consciously, chosen to ignore were the teachings that called him into a personal living relationship with Jesus—teachings that could have breathed spiritual life, depth, and vitality into his externalized moral belief system. Arlen had grown adept at pushing such anxious thoughts, or in this case questions, to the back of his mind. There they had lingered for him for the most part unconsciously. More recently, though, Arlen found them increasingly breaking into his consciousness. Striving to habituate Christian virtues, and emulate them for his children, had in the past given a measure of purpose and fulfillment to his life. This willful striving had, in recent years, slowly come to feel more like relentless hard work, unfueled by any passion.

What Arlen was finding increasingly hard to suppress was the growing malaise that over the last couple years had descended upon his marriage and life in general. As best he could recall, it had begun after he had turned thirty-eight and felt himself rapidly approaching forty and solid middle age. A mixture of boredom, the sense that he lacked some deeper meaning or purpose to his life he could not identify, and a mild but persistent despair seemed to hang over him like a dark cloud. His wife became aware of his growing despondency and tried to help him in several ways. She had advised him to seek counseling. She had also suggested he pick up an avocation that might restore some passion to his life. Aware that over the last couple of years he had been less apt to show spontaneous affection toward her, she had even suggested they break away on a second honeymoon. Arlen's wife had taught history at a local high school for over a decade. Her investment in her student's educational progress and welfare had given a measure of meaning and purpose to her life. Yet, as she approached middle age, she too began to feel like that something deeper, more holistic, perhaps even spiritual, was missing from her life.

Arlen loved his children dearly, but his work had often taken precedence overspending time with them at home and at school-related events. This left his wife with the major burden of attending these and other activities. They included soccer games, dance classes, school choral presentations, and the like. Arlen tried reassuring himself that he was essentially a good person who had not caused any significant harm to others that he could recall. In his work he had always treated his employees at the accounting firm he had started, as well as his clients, fairly and honestly. Still, it sometimes bothered him that aside from the charities he and his wife regularly, albeit modestly, gave to, he had not gone out of his way to help others, even family members. He became increasingly aware that there was nothing in his life he felt passionate about, that motivated him, on a deeper level, to feel connected to and care about others. Despite his external investment in Christian morality, and recalling his pastor's challenge during Bible study, he began to suspect that he lacked the deeper faith commitment and spiritual life that might nurture such motivation and passion within him.

He was becoming more aware of the possibility that the lack of any deeper spiritual passion within him was contributing to the growing malaise, and despair that afflicted him. He began to question whether his endless striving to live ethically really mattered in the end. The Christian values he had strived to live by no longer seemed as sanctioned and validated by his predominant understanding of God in Christ as a moral law giver.

A book he had read in college entitled *Peer Gynt*, by Henrik Ibsen, had come uncomfortably to mind more recently. In the story, its main character, Peer Gynt, on his way home to Norway, is confronted by the button molder, a figure sent by God to acquire his soul. The button molder informs Peer Gynt that his soul must be melted down and re-molded because he had failed to live an authentic and unique individual existence motivated by a passionate faith life. He was neither good enough for heaven, nor bad enough for hell. Briefly stated, in his life he had avoided any deeper passionate life commitments, be they good or bad.

Despite reassuring himself that he had tried to adhere to the most important Christian morals as best he could, if honest with himself, given the malaise he now battled, it no longer seemed to be enough. He had to admit to himself that he had been much better at practicing a list of Christian moral do nots than the Christian moral dos made possible through Christ's saving grace and informed by his greatest commandment.

As before, the commandment to love God with one's heart, mind, and soul and one's neighbor as oneself held little significance for him. Again, he had always been confused by what Jesus meant by "neighbor" in the parable of the good Samaritan. Except for an occasional wave, he hardly knew his neighbors, nor did they seem to want to become any better acquainted with him. He had once even asked his pastor about what Jesus had meant by his use of "neighbor" in the parable, but at the time he had not been able to reflect on or comprehend his answer. The increasing malaise that now gripped him had at least sparked some self-reflection in him.

It was late afternoon that Christmas Eve when Arlen arrived home from the office. Working late into the day had made attending either Christmas Eve service impossible. Taking off his coat, he turned to greet his wife who was descending the stairs. "Arlen" she asked impatiently, "you did remember to buy the new PlayStation video game player this week, didn't you?" She had asked him about this several times over the preceding weeks and each time, he had to admit sheepishly that he had forgotten to do so. Stopping dead in his tracks, shaking his head, and with a shamefaced expression he had to admit this yet again. This time his wife refused to accept his confession. "Arlen" she said, with a scolding edge to her voice, "the children will be very disappointed. Please make one final effort to find any remaining stores that might still have this gift in stock." With this, she finished walking down the stairs and passed by him in stoney silence. Wearing a long-suffering expression mixed with annoyance, she disappeared into the kitchen.

Arlen then called most of the large downtown department stores that had the best chance of still having this increasingly precious gift, but they were all sold out. To his surprise and relief, the last department store he called had one remaining PlayStation left in stock. He felt a mixture of relief and annoyance at himself for not caring enough to remember to buy the gift earlier.

Despite it being early evening on Christmas Eve, he resolved to go downtown and purchase the gift, more to avoid family fallout than anything else. Secretly, he felt the kids would survive the disappointment if they didn't receive this gift Christmas morning, especially if he belatedly promised to buy the gift for them right after Christmas. He was not as sure his wife would be so understanding. She had bought most of the children's other presents and had asked him to see to this one gift. He immediately asked the store to set the item aside at customer service for pickup. As he drove toward the city, he dreaded the traffic he anticipated encountering downtown. Arlen knew the downtown area well—and which parking garage was closest and within walking distance to the department store holding the coveted gift.

Although he had parked in this garage before, it had only been during the daytime when it was safer and more commonly used. He was aware that it wasn't located in the better part of the downtown area. Still, he was on a mission and was determined to see it through. Having fought traffic and arrived at the entrance to the garage, Arlen grabbed the ticket, let the long barrier arm lift, and drove through. There were no attendants in the adjacent booth. In fact, as Arlen parked on the first level, he noticed only a few other cars parked at a distance from one another. Other than this, the parking garage appeared deserted. Spotting an exit door in the far-left corner of the garage, he walked toward it. Once there he pushed the bar on the door, opened it and exited into the snowy cold winter night. Single-mindedly focused on the task ahead, he rounded the corner that led to the side street ahead, unaware of the traumatic event that would have a lasting, transformative impact on his life.

As Arlen came around the corner, he heard footsteps rush up behind him, accompanied by threatening yells and curses. His adrenaline surging, Arlen broke into a cold sweat. With his attackers all yelling at him at the same time Arlen had only been able to make out certain words: "Hey, where are you going?" followed by more cursing and then, "Hey, were talking to you." They then made their intent clear.

"Hand over your wallet!"

His heart felt like it was pounding out of his chest. Arlen spun around to find himself surrounded by three figures shrouded in shadow, with hoodies pulled over their heads. They sounded like and, as far as he could tell, appeared to be, teenagers. As he spun around, one of the teens jumped in front of him and yelled out, "Are you deaf—I said hand over your wallet." He followed this up with more angry threats and curses. He then brandished a knife to back up his threats. Recalling later what happened next, Arlen wished he had just complied, but with his adrenaline surging and an instinctive, defensive rage arising within him, he had shoved the teen, yelling at him to back off. They then attacked him from all sides with cruel barbarity and senseless rage. He knew it had not taken his attackers long to beat him senseless. From what he could recall of the attack, everything had seemed to move in slow motion at the time

The teen in front of him threw a sudden, wild, hard punch that nevertheless connected. It knocked Arlen to the ground and left him in a semiconscious stupor. The teens then rushed in and began attacking him from all sides. With one straddling him, raining down punches to his head and face, the others kicked his back, chest, and the sides of his head with sadistic fury.

Arlen could not recall the exact moment he fell unconscious. Other than the initial pain and terror he had experienced during the brutal attack, everything else seemed a blur. Despite many cuts and bruises, some broken ribs, and a severe concussion, Arlen was grateful later that he hadn't been stabbed, as he likely would not have survived.

The Ritualist

Abel Decker was the associate pastor of the large downtown city church. It was early evening and he was driving home. Abel had decided that tonight he would risk cutting straight over, via a side street, to reach the highway that would take him to his apartment on the outskirts of town. Normally he would have gone further up

Given his investment in practical aspects of worship leadership, he thought he would do well here. The professor's focused critiques, written in the margins of his papers, had consistently cited similar concerns. The professor had asked him, "But what is your personal understanding, and theology, here? How have the pastoral theologians we've covered influenced your personal views?" In his heart Abel knew he lacked an inner, subjective, personal relationship with Jesus Christ, and with it, a deeper spiritual appreciation of the Eucharist. He had so habituated substituting his more externalized, egocentric motivations for deeper, more holistic spiritual ones that he seldom felt the need to reflect on a mindset that precluded any deeper faith commitment. Neither had his perfunctory prayer life sparked such reflection.

For Abel, performing the duties and particularly the worship practices of ministry in ways consistent with his tradition's dogmas and doctrines was what most reassured him of both his call to ministry and the vitality of his faith. It was also the primary bond he felt with his colleagues in area churches. Abel had substituted belief in belief for a living faith where the God we know in Jesus Christ gets the last word, one of love and grace with the power to inform our thoughts and actions. This is a love that can be critically assertive while prayerfully heeding that love's hopeful purpose in Christ. Often unwitting and insidious in nature, this human substitution has been and remains one of the most dangerous, for it afflicts the church from the inside out and has been responsible for some of its most egregious offenses.

What Abel had been largely unaware of, much less able to reflect on, were two serious consequences of his stunted spiritual ministerial motivations. First and foremost, his interactions with the youth and the greater congregation, while socially skillful and even charismatic, did not reflect a spiritual passion for the Lord and faith. Most parishioners were not bothered by this, but a few had taken notice and had made remarks such as, "I wish his faith in the Lord would shine through more." What they and others had seen lacking in him was a deeper, humbler conveyance of Christ's love for others. One wise older member close to the senior pastor had confided in him that such a spiritual quality was necessary if members were to discern the difference between a Christ-centered call to ministry from one built around a cult of personality.

But it was the performative affectation with which Abel led Communion in worship where a certain spiritual disingenuousness was most evident. The deeper, louder, and holier-than-thou tone he affected when leading Communion struck many, even those who could not ascertain why, as more prideful than spiritually heartfelt. The senior pastor, among others who had noticed this, had in one of their meetings shared this with him. While offset by his gregarious personality, it had also been evident in both his youth group and shut-in ministries. A few had noticed that his faith references and prayers seemed more perfunctory and performative than reflective of a deeper, more personally integrated faith life. The homebound and hospitalized often had to remind him to pray with them. When he had remembered to pray, it had been utilized as an expedient sign that the visit was at an end, and had afforded Abel a convenient and smooth exit. The likelihood that enough congregants also lacked a deeper and more passionately lived-out faith, explained the lack of follow-up on the matter. For church political reasons, the senior pastor had let the issue go.

Second and more specifically, Abel's driving need for control and power had led him to compete with the senior pastor in numerous subtle and, at times, condescending ways. Before services he had often, always in front of others, cautioned the white-haired senior pastor not to forget to announce some important upcoming church function or special part of the service. He had also made it a point after services at the coffee hour, and with others within earshot, to point out any mistakes the pastor had made during the service, such as losing his place in his sermon notes, or forgetting to have the congregation rise at the appropriate times. Abel was always careful to conceal such remarks in indirect ways, often couching them in an affectionate teasing manner. The white-haired senior pastor, well aware of his advancing years and approaching retirement, had keenly felt these darts land and, with a painful smile, had quickly deflected attention to another topic.

In one blatant example of Abel's undermining of the senior pastor, he had secretly met with the executive officers of the church's governing committee and asked them if they would support his ambition to preach more than once a month. The executive committee immediately informed him that such a decision lay completely within the senior minister's domain and that under no circumstances would they intervene here. Abel had skulked away more out of anger and humiliation from this chastisement than from any pangs a principled conscience aroused within him by this attempted end run. Secretly, albeit with a bit less confidence, Abel still hoped that when the senior pastor retired the search committee and congregation would approach him about the position.

The senior pastor, fully aware of Abel's machinations, purposely began to keep him on a short leash and restricted to his core duties. As tension and resentment grew between them, Abel stepped up his teasing barbs and criticisms, with the senior pastor increasingly responding with aloofness and by chilling him out.

These dynamics on Abel's part were predictive as to how he would handle the scene he was about to come upon. Abel was now well into the darker, seemingly abandoned, and ominous industrial sector. As Abel drove down the side street and approached the other side of the first large parking garage, he spotted what at first appeared to be a heap of discarded clothes ahead on the sidewalk. Slowing down, he could see this was a man in an overcoat laying curled up in a fetal position, his knees drawn up into chest. With the man cast in shadow, Abel was unable to clearly see his face or any other identify features. Abel slowed down as he was about to pass by the man. His mind raced for an explanation for the scene that confronted him. He knew it was not uncommon for the homeless to sleep in various locations around the downtown area. Perhaps the man was asleep, although this seemed like a strange and unlikely place for that to happen. He did not see a heating vent that could have provided the man warmth.

Abel slowed to a near stop as he came even closer to the scene, and he knew some action, particularly given his ministerial status, was required of him. Expedient rationales came quickly to mind.

He started by reassuring himself that many of the homeless people are addicts of one kind or another. This, he told himself, may well be an alcoholic who had passed out due to over intoxication.

With the man's form largely obscured by shadow, Abel, with a surge of anxiety recalling the reported increased muggings in the area, wondered if this could be a trap. What if he got out to check on the man only for him to jump up and attack him along with others who had suddenly appeared out of the shadows.

As his car slowly rolled by the scene, Abel hated to admit to himself that despite being a pastor he felt little compassion or empathy for the man, whatever his plight. Then a practical caution he recalled from one of his pastoral theology classes conveniently distracted him from this troubling thought. The professor had remarked that, as pastors, you should always be careful to consider context before helping someone lest you enable them in some self-destructive way. If this man was an addict of some kind and came to, Abel might unwittingly be drawn into such enabling behavior. Although a wise older pastor Abel knew from a local ministerial group had modified this caution. At the gathering, when the discussion had turned to the various hands-on charities the different churches supported, Abel had proudly asserted that he would never allow himself to be used when helping others. The older pastor had counseled, with a humble authority and gravitas borne from age and life experience, that "if it is Christian love, one must be prepared to risk being used at times."

Abel's rationalizations had not totally assuaged his conscience, but they relieved it just enough for him to keep rolling by, pick up speed, and leave the scene behind. As he turned onto the main drag out of the city, he breathed a sigh of relief. Abel then dispelled any remaining pangs of conscience by calling the police on his cell phone and alerting them to the man's location and condition. The dispassionate tone of the dispatcher, did not inspire confidence that any immediate action or concerted effort would be made to check on the man's wellbeing.

His conscience largely unfettered, Abel felt freed up, once again, to anticipate the evening's pleasures. That was until the troubling thought he'd had before came fully back to mind, this time as a question. "As a Christian and a pastor, shouldn't I have felt more compassion, empathy, and humanity toward this man? Is there something missing inside of me, some spiritually malformed or uncultivated part of me?" He then countered these troubled thoughts in his head. No, devotion to a belief system and performative acts of ministry and ritual were tangible, controllable. Half-conscious of the chaos of his childhood years, and fully aware of the secular tsunami sweeping the religious landscape, he thought, "This is what is real, what works." Abel then did what had become second nature for him and once more pushed these thoughts out of his mind, focusing on the evening's pleasures that awaited.

The Legalist

Delbert had an influential role within his church and on his church governing committee. He knew the church's rules, policies, and constitution better than anyone in the church. Whenever a new initiative was presented at the governing committee, Delbert was consulted. When any point of contention arose within the governing committee or congregation, and the church's constitution needed to be consulted, Delbert's expertise was sought. At the church's annual meeting, he sat at the head table with the president, vice president, and secretary and relished his role as parliamentarian. On matters related to the constitution, Delbert almost always had the final say. No one, other than the pastor, had enough expertise to challenge his legalistic constitutional interpretations. The pastor had selectively challenged his judgements, but since Delbert was a member of one of the church's most prominent families, the pastor had mostly chosen to challenge him where his legalism infringed directly on his pastoral authority. Delbert had often been teased by family and friends, given his legalistic bent of mind, that he should have been a lawyer. Delbert took this as a compliment. A few committee members and the pastor had confidentially shared concerns with each other over the black-and-white, legalistic ways he resolved church issues. This was particularly the case where they overlapped with matters of spiritual importance and affected the church's hands-on mission causes.

A few years earlier he had headed a subcommittee charged with revising the tasks and job descriptions of church committees and the church staff. He tackled this with an anal-retentive fervor for detail that clarified and explained every committee's responsibility and staff member's job description in black-and-white terms that tolerated little dissent or alternative viewpoints. During a governing committee meeting, one member had asked him whether the committee descriptions and staff responsibilities were guidelines or inflexible rules. Delbert, clearly taking offense, had glared back at the questioner for a few awkward moments, after which his response exposed his cynical view of human nature and reactionary world view. "Without rules, contentiousness arises and the worst in people tends to come out. This is as true in the church as it is in everyday life." Delbert then unexpectedly added, in a non-sequitur way that barely cloaked his prejudice toward certain immigrant groups. "And if I might add, if this country had and upheld stricter immigration laws we wouldn't be taking in all the riffraff of the world." The senior pastor of the church had tried during this meeting to enlighten Delbert about Jesus' law of love and why the inhumanity with which such current and future laws are carried out should concern all Christians.

He had also tried explaining to him in private conversations that while institutional religious traditions, policies, and rules were important, it was the faith content of one's heart, spiritually, that breathed Christian love and humanity into their observance. It was all to no avail, as Delbert's stony silence clearly indicated to the pastor the closed nature of his worldview.

Those who knew Delbert best suspected his temperament and legalistic mindset stemmed, in part, from his parents, who descended from charter members who helped found the church. His father had headed the property committee for many years and had sought above all else to maintain and preserve the church building. He had also served for a time as church treasurer with a special interest in saving and diverting funds toward various church building projects and bemoaning the monthly offertory deficits. His mother had been a member of the worship committee as well as the choir over the years. She had repeatedly stressed the importance of traditional anthems and liturgy and had protested any changes made by choir directors during her tenure on the committee.

She had also often complained at worship committee meetings that the pastor and elders were not insisting forcefully enough that members have their children baptized and confirmed at the proper ages. This, she made clear, was critical if they were to keep the church's young people from drifting away from the church. Infant baptism, she argued, would set the parents, especially if members, on the proper course, ensuring their and their children's commitment to their church tradition. Confirmation, she claimed, would prevent their young people from drifting away from the church and tradition. She had also confided in the pastor her fear that unbaptized children, tainted by original sin, might not be allowed to enter heaven. Her pastor had explained to her that these were not scripturally based beliefs and were borne from a mixture of antiquated superstition, scriptural misunderstandings, and an institutional overemphasis on externalized religion.

Delbert, never prone to much self-reflection, had fully embraced his parents' institutional and religious biases and investments. After college and finding work as an insurance claims adjuster, he had settled down and gotten married. Delbert and his wife went on to have two children, both boys, aged eleven and fourteen. The family lived in the city's suburbs. Despite being only in his early forties, Delbert was among the most reactionary traditional members on the governing committee. He had championed and voted consistently for the preservation of institutional and worship norms. Like his mother, and despite a declining parental investment in the confirmation process and ceremony, Delbert had staunchly opposed any changes to its traditional adherence and protocol. He had also argued against any understanding of church membership other than that which required both baptism and confirmation. His traditional viewpoint here extended to potential new members from outside the church. After the hiring, a couple years prior, of an associate pastor, the now senior pastor initially sought an alliance with him to moderate Delbert's overly legalistic influence on the governing committee and congregation. The senior pastor had not found the new pastor to be a reliable ally. With his entrenched conservatism, Delbert had often found himself at odds with even the other more conservative members of the committee on such issues. The pastor, along with a majority of the committee, saw such gatekeeping restrictions as an overemphasis on ceremonial rite that did not take into consideration the inner faith life of potential new members. The pastor had tried once more to explain to Delbert Christ's teaching that it was the faith content of the heart that breathed spiritual life and vitality into such external ceremonies and not the other way around, to no avail.

Delbert had worked at the office late that Christmas Eve fine-tuning the policy of a large corporation's application for coverage. He had planned to leave early so that his family might celebrate a quiet Christmas Eve together at home. They had planned to eat dinner at precisely 6:00, allowing for more after-dinner Christmas Eve family time. It was already past that time now, and Delbert knew dinner would have to be postponed. This was sure to make his wife unhappy. He had also promised to help her prepare the dinner. Finishing his initial review of the documents, he resolved to call his wife to let her know that, despite running late, he was now headed home. Her voice on the other end had registered disappointment and hurt that on this night, of all nights, he was putting the job ahead of the family. Delbert felt conflicted; his supervisor had trusted him with this particularly important application, and he was determined to make it a top priority. Still, deep down, he knew his wife was right and, with a resigned sigh, closed the file and readied himself to leave. Delbert's office was in the heart of the downtown area and in the same city where Abel lived and the church was located. Given his job and temperament, Delbert was unusually risk averse. He had always taken the more traffic-congested and circuitous route home that avoided the more crime-ridden part of the downtown area. Feeling guilty about hurting one of the few people in his life he cared deeply about, Delbert impulsively chose, for the first time, to take the more direct route home through the shadier part of the city.

Taking the side street that ran past the front of the church, Delbert soon passed the well-lit downtown area and was headed toward the darker streets of the old industrial section of the city. Delbert had adhered to the speed limit as he approached the back of the two high-rise parking garages that faced the side street. He was driving slowly enough to spot what appeared to be a man collapsed on the sidewalk. Coming to a near stop, and allowing his car's headlights to illuminate the scene, Delbert was able to discern that the man was clearly unconscious. What appeared to be blood spatterings on the sidewalk around the man's head confirmed Delbert's fear that the man was a crime victim, most likely from a mugging. Despite his car's headlights on him, the man's head was still too shrouded in shadow for Delbert to get a clear look at his face. From what he could see, the man appeared well dressed, and Delbert guessed he came from a similar middle-class professional background to his. Even so, Delbert was surprised to find that he felt little empathy for him. His external religious motivations had not prepared him for a situation where empathy might have moved him to care for and about the man. Absent a passionate inner faith life having been nurtured within him, Delbert had found it difficult to form any deeper spiritual bonds with fellow Christians, much less with this stranger. Delbert had been brought up, and had become habituated under stress, to seek refuge in the logical external reassurances of protocols, rules, policies, and laws. This was true for him in the church, at work, and in his everyday life.

For a few moments, Delbert's professionally trained risk-averse mind assessed the situation as calmly as he could. First, as with Abel, he did not want to dally there too long in case the attackers were still nearby. The situation was a dangerous one where he might then be attacked as well. "And there's a risk," he told himself, "that by assisting him I might make his condition worse." What if the man came to and requested help in getting up?

He had read that moving a seriously injured person in some cases could injure them more or even be life threatening. "Obviously," he told himself "I don't have the emergency medical expertise to help this man." Delbert had rolled his window partially down and could now hear the man moaning. This put Delbert in a quandary. He knew, at least in principle, he should offer some comfort to the man. Yet again, he asked himself, "What if the attackers are still nearby—how could I then be of any help to the man?" He was somewhat familiar with the Good Samaritan Law and now tried to recall the part that protected a person from liability if they offered only minimal assistance to such an individual.

His habituated professional tendency toward assessing risk, combined with his inability to feel much empathy toward others, had left him anxious only about any possible legal responsibility he might have to help the man. Delbert then recalled something he had read online. It had clearly stated that in most states, including his, if you alert the authorities, you cannot be held liable in such situations. With this legal reassurance, Delbert resolved to call for an ambulance, and when he placed the call, he also explained to them that the man was likely a crime victim and that the police should be contacted as well. As Delbert slowly drove away, he sighed with relief, and assured himself that he had done the right thing, or at least the minimal right thing. After all, he had obeyed the letter of the law. What could be more important?

Mireya's Heart

If you'll recall, Mireya had left the diner and resolved to take the shortcut home through the alleyway. As she came close to the other end of the alley, which opened onto the side street, she breathed a sigh of relief anticipating the comforts of home sooner than usual. That was until she heard the violent sounds of a confrontation echoing through the narrow alleyway. Terrified, she cautiously crept toward the other end of the alley, clinging to the side wall of the garage. Once there and peering fearfully around the corner of the parking garage, she saw the crumpled figure of a man on the sidewalk, curled up in a fetal position. With a habituated tendency, nurtured and instilled in her over a lifetime, to express Christian love and empathy toward those in need regardless of background, Mireya's response was not unexpected. She was sure there were many in America and Honduras who shared such an inclination, just as there were many who didn't. It came down to an individual's inner motivation, for Christians a passionate inner faith motivation, not contingent on another's privileged status, ethnic, racial, religious, or nationalistic allegiance. Among other Christians, she found, she had felt the strongest spiritual bond, no matter the difference between them, with those who had experienced the transformative grace of God's love in Jesus Christ. It seemed to her that this, more than any other shared experience, made all the divisions and walls that separate human beings melt away.

With no sight or sound of anyone else around, with quickening steps, Mireya approached the man and, setting her purse down next to her, she knelt beside him. Grasping his hand, she whispered into his ear how sorry she was this had happened to him and that she would call for help. She had hoped for some response, a squeeze of the hand, or painful moan. With none forthcoming she became acutely aware that help could not come soon enough. Releasing his hand, while at the same time whispering to him softly and reassuringly that she was calling for help, she reached for the flip phone in her purse. She then called the police and requested that an ambulance also be sent right away. She described him in detail as a well-dressed man who was wearing a suit and expensive overcoat and was most likely a crime victim. With mixed feelings she felt her description might prompt a timelier response. Having made the call, Mireya leaned close to the man's ear again and whispered, "They are on their way." She soon heard the wail of an ambulance in the distance and knew it would not be long before they arrived. Once on the scene, the paramedics went quickly to work. They placed a brace around his neck and then laid him carefully onto a gurney and loaded him into the ambulance. The police arrived soon after the ambulance.

Overhearing that the man's wallet had been stolen, and learning that no other identifying information had been found on him, Mireya did two things she wouldn't normally consider doing. First, she asked one of the paramedics if she could ride along with him. Given the circumstances and the obvious differences in their appearance, the paramedic, wearing a suspicious expression, asked, "Are you family? Do you even know this man?" Mireya did something then that went against a Christian principle that had become part of her and second nature to her. Her father had also taught her to consider the circumstances and context of a situation before adhering too rigidly to some external moral principle. Knowing that having someone with him expressing Christian love and care might increase his chance of survival, she lied. She told the paramedic that this was a man she knew well from the diner where she worked. She then added that he had been a regular customer for some years and, in that time, they had become well acquainted and had even become friends. Against his better judgement, and knowing the man's family could not be readily contacted, the paramedic relented on condition that she sat quietly at the back of the ambulance near his feet, and not interfere in any way with emergency efforts to stabilize him. When they arrived at the emergency room, the medical personnel there quickly helped transfer him onto a medical cart. The paramedic had informed a member of the emergency crew what Mireya had done to save the man's life and that they knew each other. She had then been allowed to accompany him into the partitioned, curtained-off emergency room where he was taken. The curtains were drawn as emergency personnel, including an ER doctor, continued to work on him. Mireya had been allowed to sit quietly in a corner at the foot of the bed. After an hour or two his condition stabilized, and with only a nurse checking on him semi-regularly, Mireya had been able, much of the time, to sit by his side and hold his hand. As the hours went by, the man finally began to stir and soon after opened his eyes and, after a painful moan, asked, "Where am I?" Mireya leaned in close, and in a soft, gentle voice shared that she had come upon him at the parking garage after he had been attacked and had called for help. With his eyes now wide open and his senses beginning to clear, he responded, "I think my name is Arlen, but I have little memory of the attack." She told him that his wallet had been stolen and there had been no other identification found on him for the hospital to contact his family with. "Can you tell me who to call now?" Arlen hesitated, squinted, and furrowed his brow as he tried hard to clear the mental cobwebs that still filled his head. Recalling bits and pieces of memory, he suddenly said, "I think I have a wife and children who live in the suburbs."

"Can you remember your wife's full name or a phone number?" she asked with gentle encouragement. Grimacing with concentration and rubbing his forehead, he said, "I'll try." Then, hesitantly, he began to recall the numbers. "I think it's 507. No, 570." After more hesitation, he uttered the next three numbers in quick succession. Then after an even longer pause, and with a sigh and expression of relief, he was able to recall and say the last four numbers. Pulling a pen from her purse Mireya wrote down the phone number. As she excused herself, she saw that Arlen suddenly appeared anxious. Reassuring him she would be right back, she went to the nurses' station to pass on this critical information. Mireya informed the nurse that he was awake, and the nurse, with a pleased and relieved expression, assured Mireya she would call the family immediately. As Mireya walked back to where the man was, a nurse and a doctor rushed ahead of her into the room. Once more Mireya retreated quietly to the corner chair a couple feet from the end of the bed. Other medical personnel came and went, and additional tests were run. When all the commotion subsided, Mireya quietly moved once more to the chair next to the man, but anticipating his family's arrival, she refrained from holding his hand. Now fully awake, and with the latest dose of pain medication kicking in, Arlen turned his head on his pillow toward Mireya and with two heartfelt words and a voice choked with emotion said simply, "Thank you."

Within a half hour the curtain at the foot of Abel's bed was pulled open and Arlen's family entered. Mireya retreated again to the corner chair at the foot of his bed. Abel's wife rushed to his side. Both, with tears flowing, whispered words full of emotion and relief to each other. Mireya waited anxiously with bated breath for his wife's reaction to her, as her two children, with wide-eyed expressions, stared back and forth from their mother to her. She fully expected her to say, "And who the heck are you?" After a few minutes, Arlen's wife did look up and over at her, but what Mireya heard instead, in a voice choked with emotion and gratitude, was "How can we ever thank you?" After asking a few other questions, including how she happened to come upon Abel, she learned of the diner where Mireya worked.

Following their exchange, Mireya politely excused herself and called for a taxi to take her home. Days and then months passed, work and life routines returned to normal, which for Mireya could, in her off hours, be lonely at times. Then one sunny morning in mid-April, as Easter approached, something totally unexpected happened in Mireya's otherwise routine workday. In one of the countless times that found Mireya carrying a full tub of dishes back to the kitchen, her eye caught a family entering the diner who looked strangely familiar. As she stopped just long enough to get a better look, an expression of delighted recognition and a warm smile shone across her face. It was Arlen and his family. Once seated, and with Mireya having come back from the kitchen, they called out to her and motioned for her to come over to them. They then greeted one another as if they were old friends. Arlen asked her how she was doing, and informed her that it had been his and his wife's intention as soon as he was fully recovered to come see her at the diner. In the conversation that followed, they learned that Mireya lived alone and that the rest of her family were still back in Honduras. She informed them that she had come alone to America to earn money to send to her family back home as they struggled every day to put food on the table. The diner had been slow that morning, which enabled Arlen and Mireya to have a more prolonged conversation where he was able to tell her, in greater detail, about his recovery. Arlen and his wife had also informed the diner's owner, who happened to be at the register as they came in, of their very special reunion. Recalling the incident, he nodded, smiling in understanding agreement. As Arlen and Mireya talked on, Arlen's wife's mind began to wander. She recalled that genealogical research had revealed that a forebear of hers, a young man, had been the first to immigrate from Ireland to America during the Irish potato famine with similar hopes and dreams to Mireya's. In a letter he had written to family back home, which had later been brought over and passed on to his daughter, he shared first recollections of when his ship had pulled into the New York harbor. While he knew many challenges and troubles lay ahead, the sight of the Statue of Liberty had filled him with an irrepressible hope that somehow, with hard work, faith, and perseverance, things would be different here. As Arlen and Mireya continued to converse, her mind wandered further. She then recalled the words of poet Emma Lazarus: "Give me your tired, your poor, / Your huddled masses yearning to breathe free." Her heart sank in a moment of despondency. She couldn't help but wonder if many Americans, generations later, forgetting that we are a nation of immigrants who often had to overcome prejudice, could still be moved by these words. Even if they were, she asked herself, did they see these powerful poetic lines as applicable to all immigrants, or only select ones? As a high school history teacher, she also recalled Jefferson's words from the Declaration of Independence: "We hold these truths to be self-evident, that all men are created equal." Well aware of the cultural limitations of the time period, she knew a vision was implicit in these words that transcended its historical context. As a history teacher, she knew as well that it was precisely because of the immigrant nature of our country that a social and economic class system had not at the outset become as rooted in our culture.

Arlen suddenly broke into her stream-of-consciousness reflections and brought her attention back to the present moment. He had turned his head toward her and caught her eye with a look of serious intent. Mireya stood by unsure of what was going on. Somehow, though, Arlen's wife intuitively did. A discussion they had had in the car on their way to the diner no doubt helped. A knowing smile crept across both their faces. Both looked back at Mireya, and Arlen asked her a question that caught her totally off guard.

"Mireya what are you doing on Easter?"

"I usually attend Mass early in the day," came her hesitant and puzzled response.

Then, with determined assertiveness, Arlen said, "Mireya, we would like to invite you to our home for Easter dinner. I can pick you up after Mass at your home and bring you back later that night." Taken aback, Mireya for once stopped smiling and took a hesitant step back, unsure of what to say. After a few more moments of awkward silence, and with a shy smile, she replied, "Thank you very much, but you don't have to do this." Without missing a beat Arlen responded, saying, "We're extending this invitation with all our hearts not because we have too, but because we want to." Arlen smiled in a warm, encouraging way at Mireya and added, "Please accept our invitation. It would mean the world to us."

Arlen paused briefly carefully considering what he was about to say next. He then said, "Mireya, I am almost certain you are a person of faith, so let me share with you something I learned from this whole experience. It has become clear to me that you were not only my good Samaritan but were and are my neighbor and sister in Christ."

Arlen had finally come to understand what Jesus meant by neighbor in the good Samaritan parable. He suspected he had intuitively known its deeper meaning all along, but his experience had brought it into full consciousness and acceptance. Jesus was teaching the legal expert and us just how radically inclusive God's saving grace is. It unites us in a kingdom that disregards race, ethnicity, nationality, status, religious affiliation, and even spatial distances. In God's kingdom we all become neighbors. We are a universal family brought to fruition through Christ's death and resurrection. By consequence, all who cross our path in need can be considered our neighbor—prayer, the work of the Spirit, and Christian love closing whatever the perceived distance and nurturing our spiritual bond with them. They may be someone in need we literally come upon at the crossroads of life, like Mireya had with him, or those in need brought into our consciousness. Given that we are all continually in need of God's love in Christ, everyone can potentially be seen as our neighbor. During and following his recovery, Arlen's heartfelt prayers, devotions, and Bible study had fostered transformative spiritual growth in him. Along the way, he had learned another important lesson: that all who hold Christ in their heart hold dual citizenship. One in the land to which we belong, and the other in God's heavenly kingdom on earth through the work of the Holy Spirit. God's kingdom, unlike secular citizenship, does not impose legalities upon us, draw boundaries around us, or stir up prejudice among us. Its currency is the grateful sharing of that love and its transformative grace, which Christ first gifted us, with others in a radically inclusive way. These were reflections and insights Arlen had had during his recovery and before his conversation with Mireya at the diner.

Shaking her head in recognition of what Arlen had said, Mireya had responded confidently, "I would be very happy to join your family this Easter. Thank you so very much for including me on this very special day for faith and family." A few more words were exchanged, which included Mireya sharing her address and phone number with them. Arlen's wife wrote these down carefully. With the conversation at an end, Mireya picked up her tub of dishes, smiled warmly one last time back at Arlen and his wife, and slowly disappeared into the kitchen.

In the week before Easter, preparations were made for the Easter dinner that now included Mireya. Neither party knew this yet, but she was to become part of the family and part of numerous other special occasions and holidays in their family's life. Arlen and his wife and children came to love her as well. More importantly, they had both learned through Mireya's example what Jesus meant when he taught us to love our neighbor.

A Seed Is Planted

With these words the older gray-haired man telling this story to the young man at the cafe paused, and took a long sip from what was left in his large cup of coffee. Looking directly into the young man's eyes, he said, "Well, that's the whole story. Did that help you understand any better what our Lord meant by neighbor?"

A broad, eager smile broke across the young man's face. "So the good Samaritan was Mireya?" But then as he cocked his head up and to one side his expression changed to a doubtful frown, and he said, "I still have trouble, though, accepting how someone who looks so different from us and is not even an American could be considered my neighbor? What could we possibly share that would qualify her as a neighbor?"

The older man leaned forward, slowly lifted his head, and looked directly into the young man's eyes with a knowing smile and said patiently, "God's saving love does not wear blinders." He then added, "While prayer and the guidance of the Holy Spirit may be necessary to discern how best to share that love with others, it should never exclude anyone based on race, ethnicity, status, religion, or nationality." He continued, "You see, in God's eyes we are all God's children, equally loved, equally sought, and equally valued. With hearts overflowing with gratitude for God's saving transformative love in our life, we are not just inspired by the Holy Spirit to love God, but to share that love with others, in a radically inclusive way that embraces all of humanity."

"But I still don't get it," the young man said. "That's totally unrealistic. Our world is divided by all those things you just discounted, particularly nationality. How can we just ignore all that? Seems to me wanting to hold onto such loyalty is just part of human nature. Besides, I am proud to be an American; it seems like you're asking me to forget all this means to me."

The older man then answered him in a tone that conveyed empathy, but also a resolve to instruct. "I understand what you're saying, but you're confusing God's heavenly kingdom with our earthly kingdoms. It's okay to hold such loyalties as long as they don't conflict with the most essential loyalties we owe God. While God extended his heavenly kingdom to us through Jesus Christ, it also transcends this world and is not of this world. This kingdom finds its most radical expression when it comes up against worldly authorities and powers that oppose the sharing of this radically inclusive love. It is at such times that our dual citizenship becomes most challenging and we feel most conflicted. It is then that God's heavenly kingdom becomes a kingdom against earthly authorities, powers, and kingdoms. To conflate God's heavenly kingdom with a worldly one is to become part of the opposition to God's plan to manifest God's heavenly kingdom on earth through Jesus Christ. We are in danger then of lowering God's status to that of a state deity and not the awe-inspiring, transcendent God we know only partly in Jesus Christ. You see, it is God's plan to reveal his heavenly kingdom on earth through acts of Christian love both as individuals and as a movement. With the prayerful assistance of the Holy Spirit, that love can express itself in many ways, including the offering of life's staples to those in need, forgiveness, reconciliation, and emotional and spiritual support. It can also take the form, when necessary, of an unwavering, assertive, active resistance to those who would compromise, corrupt, and oppress those who would share that love, or who are desperately in need of it."

At this the young man lowered his head, and then slowly raising it looked directly back into the older man's eyes. He then nodded his head slowly and with an acquiescent smile said, "You know how much I respect you and appreciate the time and care you've invested in me. Also, if honest, your faith has a lived-out, authentic quality that I've felt drawn to. Still, this is a lot for me to swallow, at least right now. It goes against much of what I was taught growing up and have since become emotionally invested in. I must say, though, the story you just told is a powerful one and illustrates well what I think you're trying to get me to understand."

Then tilting his head up and looking suspiciously at the older man, he suddenly paused once again. "Wait a minute." He asked with a wry smile, "How do you know this story is even true? I see how the story shares parallels with the parable of the good Samaritan, but how do you know whoever passed it on to you told it the way it really happened, or that they didn't make the whole thing up?"

"Couldn't it still convey a deeper spiritual truth as does the parable of the good Samaritan that Jesus told?" the older man responded, suspecting this would not satisfy the younger man's need for a more concrete provenance.

The older man then smiled and looked discerningly into the young man's eyes. He was keenly aware of the young man's closed worldview and resistance to any new perspective that challenged it. And yet the older man sensed a receptiveness in the young man's voice he hadn't heard before. A few further moments of awkward silence ensued during which the older man continued to look at the young man, unsure of how what he was about to share would go over. Would he see him differently, or lose respect for him? He knew, whether warranted or not, that the deeply ingrained nature of the young man's suspicion left him with little choice. Without breaking eye contact the older man sat back in his chair. Then with solemn and dramatic emphasis on nearly every word, he broke the silence and made his confession: "Because I was Arlen, the man attacked in the story. I was that man!"

The smirk evaporated from the young man's face, and he stared back at him incredulously. "I don't understand. Your name's not Arlen, it's Arthur or Art."

"I changed my name hoping you would consider the story on its own merit, and later arrive at your own conclusions. I had been praying to plant a seed of truth within you that, with further reflection and more life experience, you might then internalize and claim subjectively as your own. Still, I did not want to let any doubt about the story's validity linger in your mind, so I decided to come clean."

"There's one more thing I must tell you. Before I had this traumatic experience as a young man, I too had heard a sermon on the parable of the good Samaritan. After the service I could see that the pastor was still in the back of the church. He had just finished talking with a parishioner and had slowly begun to walk back toward his office. Aware that my faith commitment was superficial and defined more by what I shouldn't do than what I should do as a Christian, an anxious thought had arisen within me at times. If there was an afterlife, would my nominal Christian faith be enough to get me into heaven? So, I walked up to the pastor, not unlike the man in the parable, and asked him about this. He smiled at me warmly and told me that he appreciated the question. First, he cautioned me that it is God alone who knows the depths of the human heart, and it is God's divine love and judgement that has the final say here, not us. He went on to explain how God's law of love had fulfilled all the Law and the Prophets. For many Christians, he told me, it is in living out the truth of this greatest commandment, centered prayerfully in Christ's Spirit and in faith and gratitude for God's saving love, that we share in God's promise of eternal life. As an aside, he added that it is through the lens of this commandment that all Scripture should be prayerfully viewed and interpreted. Part of living out that truth, he added, is sharing God's love and grace with all those in the greater Christian neighborhood we call the world. I now know that he was not assuming that everyone in the world was a Christian, just that in God's eyes we are all his children and his love does not discriminate, and neither should ours. He then summed up his answer to my question succinctly by paraphrasing Jesus' answer, 'Seek prayerfully to love the God we know in Jesus Christ, and your neighbor as yourself, and you will live.'

"At the time I could grasp that prayer might help get me closer to the God I knew of in Jesus Christ, even if I wasn't ready to put it into practice. What I didn't understand, and wasn't ready to understand, was what the pastor and Jesus meant by 'neighbor.' Still, he planted a seed in me, although it took the experience, I just shared for it to germinate."

The younger man shook his head and smiled acknowledging parallels between their faith journeys. Then, wearing a more serious expression, he repeated that it would take him some time to process all that had just been shared. Even so, the older man once again sensed a receptivity in the younger man's tone and manner that gave him hope that a seed had been planted in him that day. They then sat together for a time in comfortable silence and finished drinking their coffee.

A seed had indeed been planted in the young man that day. Experience, a further nurturance into the faith by mature Christians, and a prayerful openness to the cultivating work of the Spirit would all be necessary for this seed to germinate. The older man, as with the apostles Peter and Paul, had not so much tried to coerce another into the faith. He had simply shared a story, or, as it turns out, his story, his faith journey and spiritual transformation. He had then let the young man raise any questions he had. The truth at the heart of his story and the parable of the good Samaritan, once subjectively owned and lived out, permits no compromising, corrupting allegiance to status, nation, race, ethnicity, religious tradition, or spatial separation.

It liberates us to share the love of Christ with all those in need of God's love in Christ. We may meet them literally at the crossroads of everyday life or in our growing consciousness of the plight of others, even those at a distance, who we're able to help. The most shocking, and often misunderstood, element of the story is that the good Samaritan and our neighbor may be who we least expect it to be. It might just be someone like Mireya Zelaya Portillo.

www.ingramcontent.com/pod-product-compliance
Lightning Source LLC
LaVergne TN
LVHW010546100826
845148LV00013B/2624

* 9 7 9 8 3 8 5 2 7 5 7 7 9 *

According to A.W. Tozer many people call themselves Christians because they accept certain beliefs about Christ, yet have never come to experience the transforming reality of His love.[1]